THE GOLDEN BOOK OF
WORDS

by Selma Lola Chambers

illustrated by Louis Cary

A GOLDEN BOOK • NEW YORK

Western Publishing Company, Inc., Racine, Wisconsin 53404

INTRODUCTION

It is fascinating for very young children to associate a word with its pictorial representation.

In THE GOLDEN BOOK OF WORDS, each small picture represents a specific word. The pictures are arranged in groups—The Family, Things That Grow, Things That Go, Numbers, and so forth. Children will enjoy finding pictures of familiar objects and activities.

THE GOLDEN BOOK OF WORDS is intended for use by children who are just learning to read. They will soon begin to associate the written symbols with the pictures.

This book offers many opportunities for games of word recognition and spelling. If left to the spontaneous use of young children, it is likely to lead to a great variety of activities.

The Family

grandfather

father

mother

grandmother

brother

baby

sister

People

he

she

man

woman

children

they

girl

boy

More
People

postman

neighbor

fireman

policewoman

teacher

ice-cream
man

friends

Colors

red

black

purple

yellow

blue

orange

brown

green

pink

gray

white

Things to Play With

horn

balloon

sled

jump rope

truck

drum

teddy bear

wagon

kite

doll

ball

puzzle

train

blocks

marbles

roller skates

tricycle

Clothes

earmuffs

skirt

shirt

snowsuit

pajamas

rubbers

mittens

boots

suit

socks

slippers

overalls

hat

coat

dress

underwear

shoes

sweater

pants

gloves

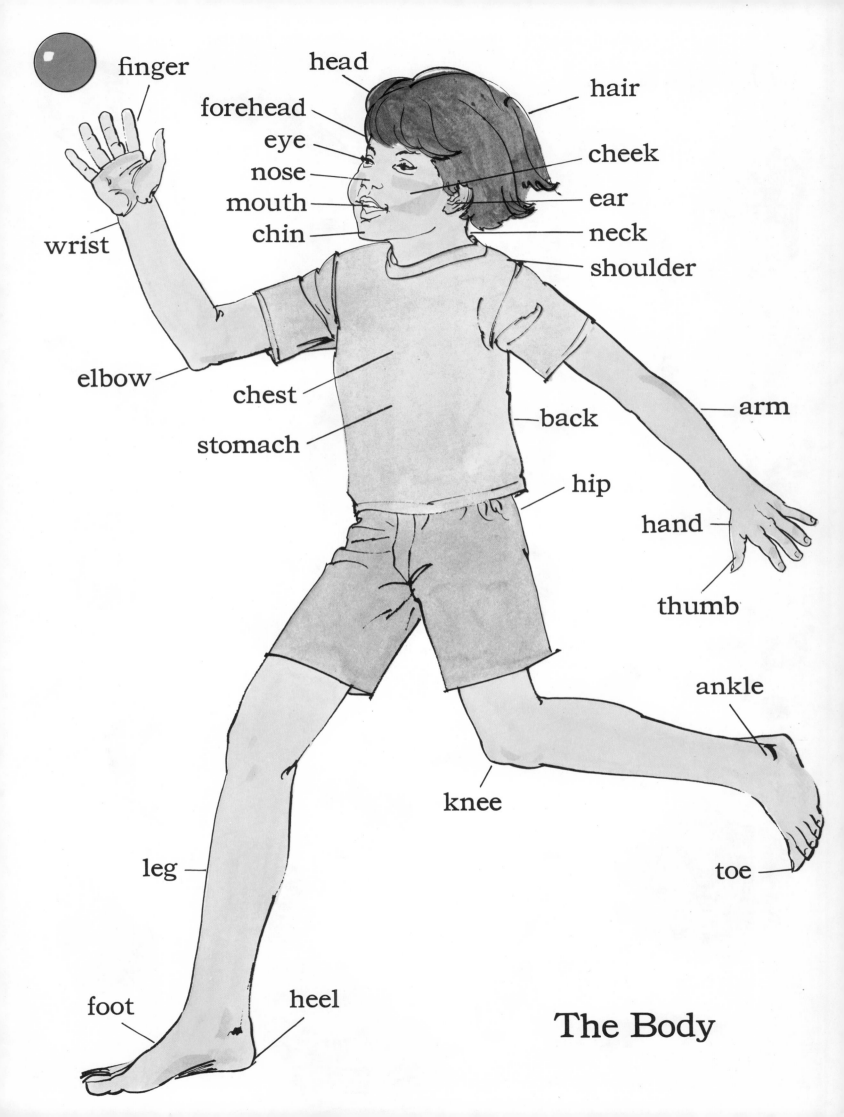

finger

head

hair

forehead

eye

cheek

nose

ear

mouth

neck

chin

shoulder

wrist

elbow

arm

chest

back

stomach

hip

hand

thumb

ankle

knee

leg

toe

foot

heel

The Body

Things to Eat

eggs

carrot

apple

milk

cake

orange

cheese

potato

jelly

corn

celery

tomato

grapefruit

peach

candy

banana

cookies

meat

lettuce

bread and butter

grapes

pear

ice cream

pancakes

Things That Grow

strawberry

tree

flower

bush

weed

tree

corn

fern

vine

grass

Things We Do

jump

write

dance

work

build

run

swing

walk

read

draw

blow

swim

crawl

sleep

eat

Things We Use

spoon

glass

pan

dishes

scissors

paper

knife

fork

broom

table

chair

iron

clock

crayons

comb

pencil

hairbrush

toothbrush

soap

radio

paintbrush

book

telephone

paints

box

television

towel

Things That Go

rocket

airplane

tractor

taxi

car

truck

trailer truck

motorboat

fire engine

bus

helicopter

train

steamship

Places to Go

home

movies

beach

park

school

country

yard

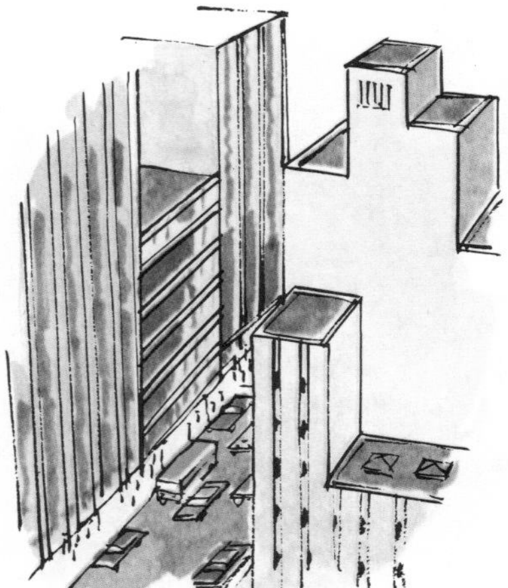

museum

city

store

friend's house

zoo

church

Zoo Animals

monkey

bear

fox

giraffe

deer

elephant

lion

hippopotamus

turtle

snake

Farm Animals

goat

horse

sheep

cat

cow

pig

dog

Birds

owl

parrot

robin

hen

duck

pigeon

turkey

crow

sparrow

eagle

canary

Word Helpers

to the store

from the store

stop

go

in the house

out
of the house

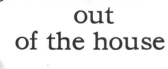

over the fence

under the fence

empty

full

up the stairs

down the stairs

socks on

socks off

raining

not raining

before the haircut

after the haircut

many fish

few fish

old shoes

new shoes

Shapes and Sizes

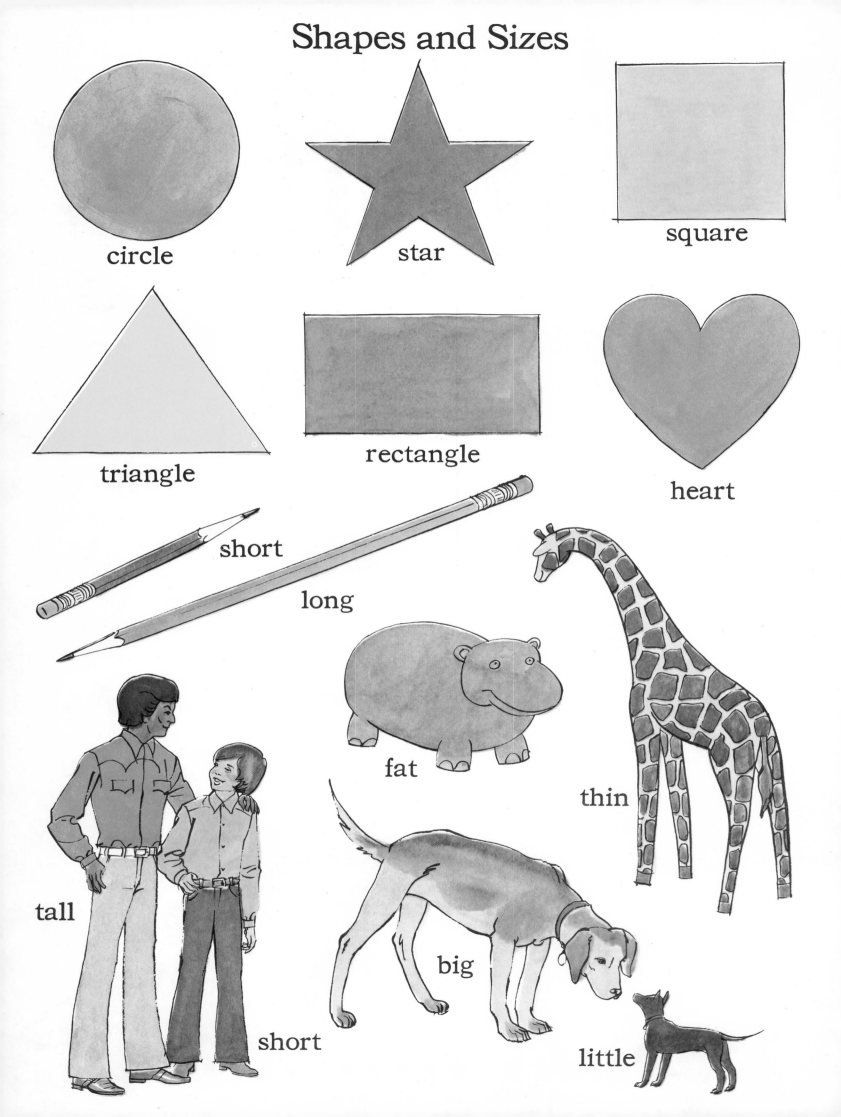

circle

star

square

triangle

rectangle

heart

short

long

short

tall

fat

big

little

thin

Numbers

1 one

2 two

3 three

4 four

5 five

6 six

7 seven

8 eight

9 nine

10 ten

11 eleven

12 twelve

13 thirteen

14 fourteen

15 fifteen

16 sixteen

17 seventeen

18 eighteen

19 nineteen

20 twenty

MY BIG GOLDEN
COUNTING BOOK

By LILIAN MOORE
Pictures by GARTH WILLIAMS

A GOLDEN BOOK • NEW YORK
Western Publishing Company, Inc., Racine, Wisconsin 53404

1

One little puppy,
A roly-poly puppy, alone as he can be.
"Isn't there a boy or girl
Who wants to play with me?"

Two little woolly lambs
Looking for their mother.
Two little woolly lambs,
A sister and a brother.

Mother Horse
And Daddy Horse
Are proud as they can be...

Because they have a baby horse
And baby horse makes three.

Four furry, purry kittens
Look alike because

Each furry, purry kitten
Has four white paws.

5

Bunny finds five cabbages
Near the garden wall.
Bunny sniffs five cabbages,
And Bunny wants them all
One, two, three, four, five.

One, two, three,
Four, five, six.
First they were eggs...

Now, they are chicks!

Waddle, waddle, waddle,
The baby ducklings go,
Waddling after Mother Duck,
Seven in a row.

7

Swish, swish,
Eight fish
Swimming in the brook…

Swish, swish,
Wise fish,
Swimming past the hook.

High in the sky
In the shape of a "V"
How many wild geese
Can you see?

Hurry and count them
As they fly.
You will see nine geese,
And so will I!

How many nuts did you find,
Little Squirrel,
Looking high and low?
Chitter, chatter,
What's the matter?
Don't you know?
Little Squirrel, I'll tell you, then.
Little Squirrel, you found ten.

10

Five butterflies at rest.
Five butterflies at play.

Here comes kitty.
What a pity.
Now all ten fly away.

They don't waddle, they don't fly—
Which ones can they be?
Can you find them, can you count them—
There are only three.

They do not bark, they don't say peep—
Which ones can they be?
Can you find them, can you count them—
There are only four to see.

THE BIG GOLDEN
ANIMAL ABC

THE BIG GOLDEN
ANIMAL A B C

by Garth Williams

A GOLDEN BOOK • NEW YORK
Western Publishing Company, Inc.
Racine, Wisconsin 53404

A a

for ALLIGATOR

B b

for BEAR

Cc

for CAT

D d

for DEER

E e
for ERMINE

F f

for FISH

G g

for GIRAFFE

H h  for HORSE

I i **for IBIS**

J j for **JAGUAR**

K k for **KANGAROO**

L l for LADYBUG

M m for MOUSE

N n for NIGHTINGALE

O o for OSTRICH

P p for PANDA

Q q

for QUAIL

R r for ROOSTER

S s

for SEAL

T t for TURTLE

U u for UNICORN

V v for VULTURE

W w for WALRUS

X x
for XENURUS

Y y   for YAK